A Kitten Called Moonlight

For Charlotte

M. W.

For Elizabeth

C. B.

First published 2000 by Walker Books Ltd
87 Vauxhall Walk, London SE11 5HJ

10 9 8 7 6 5 4 3 2 1

Text © 2000 Martin Waddell
Illustrations © 2000 Christian Birmingham

This book has been typeset in Calligraphic.

Printed in Italy

British Library Cataloguing in Publication Data
A catalogue record for this book
is available from the British Library.

ISBN 0-7445-8261-X

Martin Waddell

A Kitten Called Moonlight

Illustrated by

Christian Birmingham

WALKER BOOKS
AND SUBSIDIARIES

LONDON · BOSTON · SYDNEY

"I'd like my story again," Charlotte said.
"Which story?" asked Mummy.
"The one I like best, about Moonlight
   and me," Charlotte said.
"I thought that's the one it might be,"
   Mummy said.

"Once there was a white kitten called Moonlight," Mummy said.

"We don't know he was called Moonlight," Charlotte said.
"We just know he got lost."

"That's right," Mummy said, "the little kitten was lost and alone, and wandering about. It was a cold winter night."

"The little kitten was crying," said Charlotte. "Maybe he wanted someone to find him."

"Maybe he did. We don't know.
Then a big something came."

"It was a car," Charlotte said.

"I expect the little kitten had never
seen a car before," Mummy said.
"He was scared and he hid. The car
lights shone into the dark. And
there were two shiny bright eyes.
Somebody saw them."

"I know who saw them!"
said Charlotte.

"It was a little girl," Mummy said. "She had been to a party. The little girl told her mummy she had seen something move in the dark."

"'There's something down there by the boats'," Charlotte said. "That's what the little girl told her mummy."

"Yes," Mummy said. "But her mummy hurried her into the house. She didn't want her to catch cold."

"What happened then?" asked Charlotte.

"The little girl had her supper and her mummy put her to bed. Later she came to see if the little girl was asleep."

"But the little girl's bed was empty," said Charlotte. "The duvet was thrown right back, and the little girl wasn't there. 'My goodness, where can she be?' thought her mummy."

"Something like that," Mummy said. "Her mummy searched all over the house."

"I like this bit," Charlotte said.

"She found the little girl curled up by the window, gazing out at the dark sea and the moonlight that shone on the shore. 'What are you doing up out of bed?' asked her mummy."

"'There is something down there by the sea. I *know* that there is.' That's what the little girl told her mummy," said Charlotte.

"Yes she did," Mummy said, "and her mummy didn't believe there was. But she thought for a bit and said, 'We'll take a look to make sure.'"

"The little girl and her mummy went down to the shore." Charlotte said.

"Yes," Mummy said. "They searched and they searched but they couldn't find anything. 'Something *was* here,' said the little girl."

"She knew she was right," Charlotte said.

"Yes," Mummy said. "But her mummy still didn't believe her. She told the little girl, 'We'll take one more look, just in case.'"

"The little girl and her mummy walked out on the rocks. There was only the moonlight to see by. They walked right out by the edge of the sea – and what do you think they saw there?"

"It was a kitten!" said Charlotte.

"A little white kitten," said Mummy, "all thin and bony and cold. It was on a stone with the sea splashing round it. The poor little kitten was hungry and scared. The little girl and her mummy got splashed. But they rescued the kitten..."

"…and the little girl carried him
all the way home."

"She gave the kitten some warm milk and he went to sleep in her arms. And after a while the little girl felt sleepy too, and her mummy carried her and the kitten upstairs. She tucked the little girl in her bed all cosy and—"

"You've forgotten the best bit,"
said Charlotte. "Her mummy said
if no one owned the kitten they
could keep him for ever. She said
they should find a good name for
the kitten and the little girl knew
straightaway what it should be.
'Moonlight would be a good name,'
she told her mummy. 'We'd never
have found him without the
moonlight.'"

"So that's what they called their
kitten," Mummy said. "Now you've
told me the end of your story."

"We love that story, don't we Moonlight?"
Charlotte said.

"And I know why," said Mummy.

"We love it because it is about us,"
Charlotte said. "Moonlight
and Mummy and me."